NATURAL WONDERS OF THE WORLD

NIAGARA FALLS

by Lisa M. Bolt Simons

FOCUS READERS

FOCUS READERS

WWW.FOCUSREADERS.COM

Focus Readers is distributed by North Star Editions:
sales@northstareditions.com | 888-417-0195

Produced for Focus Readers by Red Line Editorial.

Content Consultant: Jeffrey R. Walker, PhD, Professor of Earth Science, Vassar College

Photographs ©: GummyBone/iStockphoto, cover, 1; CPQ/Shutterstock Images, 4–5; Red Line Editorial, 7, 13; Carol M. Highsmith/Carol M. Highsmith's America/Library of Congress, 9; Vinicius Cunha/Shutterstock Images, 10–11; ndenbak/iStockphoto, 15; kellyjnsn/Shutterstock Images, 16–17; nwbob/iStockphoto, 19; Phill Doherty/Shutterstock Images, 21; Lidiia Kozhevnikova/Shutterstock Images, 22–23; Cory Woodruff/Shutterstock Images, 25; MarcPo/iStockphoto, 27; SF photo/Shutterstock Images, 29

ISBN
978-1-63517-516-5 (hardcover)
978-1-63517-588-2 (paperback)
978-1-63517-732-9 (ebook pdf)
978-1-63517-660-5 (hosted ebook)

Library of Congress Control Number: 2017948090

Printed in the United States of America
Mankato, MN
November, 2017

ABOUT THE AUTHOR

Lisa M. Bolt Simons is a writer who has published more than 30 books with more on the way. She's also been a teacher for more than 20 years. Her fiction and nonfiction has been recognized with awards and grants. She lives in Minnesota.

TABLE OF CONTENTS

CHAPTER 1

THREE FALLS IN ONE

A cool mist from Niagara Falls sprays the boat's passengers. Atop the falls, more visitors take in the view from walkways along the falls' edge. Another walkway guides visitors to the base of the falls. No matter where they're viewed from, the falls' awesome size and power is a sight to see.

A boat helps visitors get an up-close view of Horseshoe Falls.

The Niagara River runs from Lake Erie to Lake Ontario. Midway between the two lakes, the river heads toward the falls. Approximately 757,500 gallons (2,867,450 L) of water rushes over the falls every second. This **volume** is the largest of any waterfall in North America.

Niagara Falls is actually three waterfalls. The river splits around Goat Island. To one side is Horseshoe Falls. Shaped like a horseshoe, it is the biggest of the three falls. The **brink** of this waterfall stretches 2,200 feet (670 m) across. American Falls and Bridal Veil Falls are on the other part of the river. American Falls has slight curves. Its brink is 850 feet (260 m) across. Bridal Veil Falls is straight across, with a brink of only 50 feet (15 m). The river becomes one again after the falls.

MAP OF THE FALLS

The Niagara River drops approximately 185 feet (56 m) at Niagara Falls. At American and Bridal Veil Falls, the water tumbles 70 to 110 feet (21 to 34 m). The height differs because of rock piles at the bottom. Horseshoe Falls is more dramatic. The water here drops the full 185 feet.

THREE FALLS, TWO COUNTRIES

The Niagara River is the border between Canada and the United States. Horseshoe Falls is in Canada. American Falls and Bridal Veil Falls are in the United States. Goat Island separates Horseshoe Falls from the other two falls. The much smaller Luna Island separates American Falls and Bridal Veil Falls.

American Falls (front) is in New York, and Horseshoe Falls (back) is in Canada.

Some believe the word *Niagara* comes from the Iroquois language. The word *onguiaahra* appears on early maps and could mean "**strait**." The Niagara River, then, was once called the Niagara Strait. Others believe Niagara means "thundering waters."

CHAPTER 2

ICE AGE LEGACY

During the most recent ice age, ice more than 2 miles (3.2 km) thick covered the area now known as Niagara Falls. The ice slowly moved south. As it melted, the ice became lake water. The ice completely melted approximately 12,500 years ago. The water became Lake Erie, the Niagara River, and Lake Ontario.

Ice forms at Niagara Falls during the winter.

Then the Saint Lawrence River was formed, leading to the Atlantic Ocean.

Water once ran from Lake Erie to Lake Ontario in five different places. Eventually, water ran into Lake Ontario in only one place. This location became the original Horseshoe Falls. However, it was originally 7 miles (11 km) north of its current location.

For thousands of years, the Niagara River **eroded** the **bedrock**. The bedrock was 400 million years old. Four miles (6.4 km) upriver from the original site of the falls, the river crossed an old buried riverbed. It was 25,000 years old. The water swirled around in this old riverbed.

NIAGARA FALLS HEIGHT COMPARISON

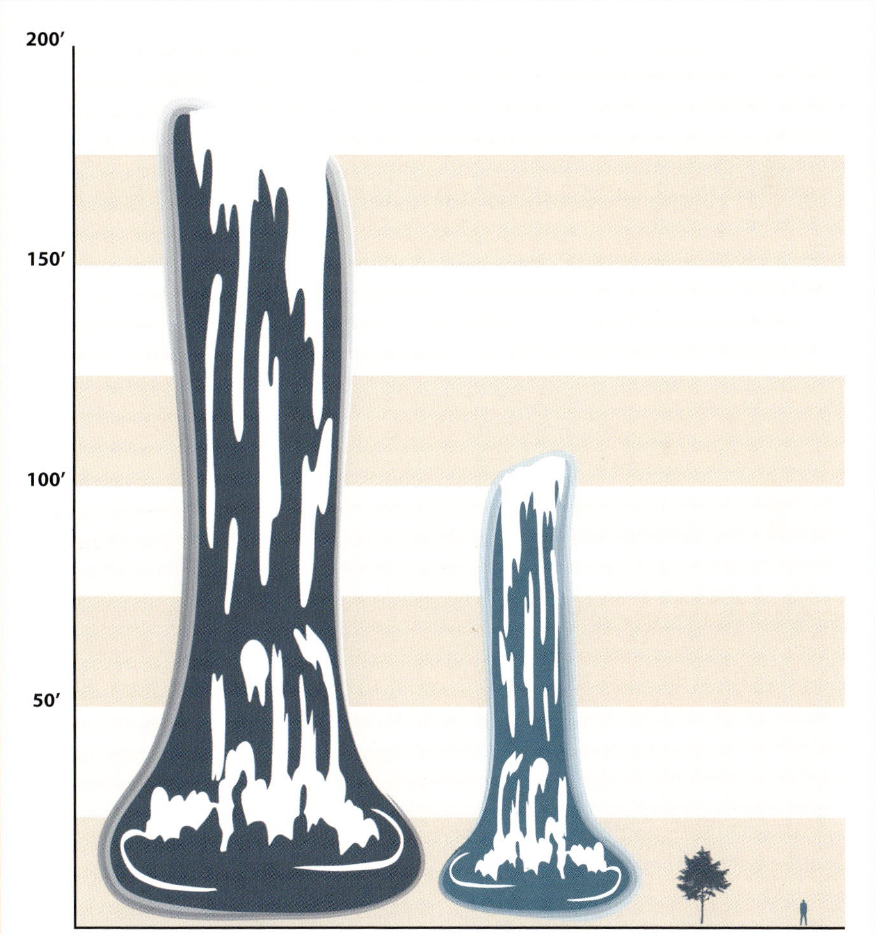

Eventually a 90-degree turn formed. This turn is now known as the Whirlpool.

The river between the falls and the Whirlpool is known as Whirlpool Rapids. Park officials consider these rapids to be the longest course of constant waves in North America. The water can rush up to 30 feet (9.1 m) per second.

THE WHIRLPOOL

The Whirlpool turns both ways. When the flow is normal, the water turns counterclockwise. Then it races into the gorge called the Devil's Hole Rapids. At night, some of the water is taken from the river to be used for **hydroelectricity**. With this slower flow, the water turns clockwise before entering the gorge.

The swirling waters at the Whirlpool are too dangerous for most boats.

The Niagara River continued to erode the bedrock for another 3 miles (4.8 km). The 7-mile (11-km) stretch from the original falls to its current location is called Niagara Gorge. At the head of this gorge are the three falls that make Niagara Falls what it is today.

CHAPTER 3

IMPORTANT AND RARE

The Niagara Falls area is home to many birds. Some make their home there. Others stop during **migration**. The National Audubon Society helps take care of birds and other wildlife. In 1996, it named the Niagara River region as an important bird area (IBA). This IBA is recognized around the world.

A seagull soars above the water at American Falls.

Peregrine falcons and American bald eagles soar across the sky at Niagara Falls. In the spring, different kinds of herons live there. On Goat Island, there is a community of ring-billed gulls. Bats fly in the falls area as well, although they are mammals and not birds.

The Niagara River is home to various types of fish. These include salmon, smallmouth bass, and trout. Lake sturgeons also live in the Niagara River. However, this fish is **endangered**. People must follow rules when fishing for it.

The fox squirrel is rare in New York. But it lives in the Niagara Falls area. Other land animals include opossums,

Lake sturgeons can grow to be 6 feet (1.8 m) long and 200 pounds (91 kg).

raccoons, and moles. Salamanders, turtles, and frogs make their homes here as well.

The Niagara Gorge is an ideal home for plants, too. Scientists have found more than 1,200 plant **species** in the region. Many of these plants grow on Goat Island. More than 600 varieties of plants have been found there. These include the rare four-leaved milkweed and the maidenhair spleenwort. Various types of trees also grow on Goat Island. These include the sugar maple, the white pine, and the black cherry.

Fourteen of the plant species found in the Niagara Gorge are rare. These include the pawpaw and fairy wand. Some of these rare plants are endangered.

Hiking trails around Niagara Falls allow visitors to see different plants and animals.

Visitors can see many of these plants and animals up close. Hiking or biking trails run throughout the park.

CHAPTER 4

WILL EROSION BE THE END?

Niagara Falls State Park is the oldest state park in the United States. The New York government approved it in 1885. Frederick Law Olmsted designed the park a year later. He wanted to protect the landscape and the shoreline for the public to enjoy.

To avoid getting wet, visitors often wear rain protection when going near the falls.

State parks limit private development. This ensures the parks are there for the public to use. Other laws have also helped protect the area. In 2008, the US government created the Niagara Falls National Heritage Area. With this bill, individuals and organizations agreed to protect the park.

Today, people who visit Niagara Falls have many options to explore. They can tour the visitors' center or view the aquarium. They can take a trolley ride or climb an observation tower. Wooden walkways lead visitors to Cave of the Winds at the bottom of Bridal Veil Falls.

A trolley takes visitors over the Whirlpool.

Guests can take helicopter rides. They can also choose between a variety of boat rides. Steel boats with diesel engines take visitors to the bottom of the falls. Jet boats zoom through fast, **Class 5 rapids**. Paddle-wheel boats take passengers on slow rides down the river.

As tourists enjoy the sites, natural erosion continues. The falls once eroded approximately 4 feet (1.2 m) per year. People have modified the river's flow so it now erodes 12 inches (30 cm) each year. But more changes aim to decrease this to less than 12 inches every 10 years.

Nature could affect the falls in other ways. Continued erosion will eventually move the falls to the outlet of Lake Erie.

LANDSCAPE PRESERVATION

Frederick Law Olmsted helped create many parks, both in cities and around natural wonders. Olmsted designed Central Park in New York City. He was also involved in developing Yosemite Valley in California.

Conservation efforts aim to protect Niagara Falls for generations to come.

This could take as long as 50,000 years. But when it happens, the Niagara River would likely become a long rapid between the two great lakes.

POWER PRODUCER

Since 1896, the strong water flow in the Niagara River has been used to create power. This is called hydroelectricity. Five main power plants are on the Niagara River. Two are in the United States, and three are in Canada.

On the US side, tunnels lead water to a bay. Water goes into the power plant. It flows down to a turbine. The turbine turns, and it spins a generator. The generator creates electricity. A transformer converts the electricity for use. On the Canada side, water leaves the Niagara River and goes into three tunnels and the Welland River. From the Welland River, the water heads to the power plant through a 12-mile (19-km) canal.

Today, the power plants on the Niagara River can produce more than four million kilowatts of

The Robert Moses Niagara Hydroelectric Power Station provides electricity to many people in New York.

electricity at any given time. This electricity can light more than 48 million 100-watt light bulbs.

FOCUS ON
NIAGARA FALLS

Write your answers on a separate piece of paper.

1. Write a letter to a friend that details what you learned about the waterfalls in Niagara Falls State Park.

2. Which of the three falls would you most like to visit? Why?

3. What separates Horseshoe Falls from the other two falls?

> **A.** Devil's Hole Rapids
> **B.** Luna Island
> **C.** Goat Island

4. What might happen if there were not specific rules for fishing for lake sturgeons?

> **A.** Lake sturgeons might become overpopulated.
> **B.** Lake sturgeons might become extinct.
> **C.** Lake sturgeons might change habitats.

Answer key on page 32.

GLOSSARY

bedrock
The layer of solid rock under soil.

brink
The edge of something high up.

Class 5 rapids
The level below the most dangerous level of rapids. These might include steep drops, fast currents, and obstacles.

endangered
In danger of dying out.

eroded
Wore away slowly over time.

hydroelectricity
Electricity that is generated by flowing water.

migration
When animals move to a different location, usually as the seasons change.

species
A group of animals or plants that are similar.

strait
A narrow waterway connecting two large bodies of water.

volume
The amount or quantity of something.

TO LEARN MORE

BOOKS

Malaspina, Ann. *What's Great about New York?* Minneapolis: Lerner Publications, 2015.

Rowell, Rebecca. *The 12 Most Amazing American Natural Wonders*. North Mankato, MN: 12-Story Library, 2015.

Stine, Megan. *Where Is Niagara Falls?* New York: Grosset & Dunlap, 2015.

NOTE TO EDUCATORS

Visit **www.focusreaders.com** to find lesson plans, activities, links, and other resources related to this title.

INDEX

Answer Key: 1. Answers will vary; **2.** Answers will vary; **3.** C; **4.** B